A Letter from Dominick the Mouse

Written and designed by Daniela Elena

Illustrated by Tasha Derossett

A division of Manifold Grace Publishing House, LLC

A Letter from Dominick the Mouse
Copyright © 2016 Daniela Elena

Illustrations: Tasha Derosett

ISBN: 978-1-937400-66-8

Printed in the United States of America

Published by PeeWee Press
A division of Manifold Grace Publishing House, LLC
Southfield, Michigan 48033
www.manifoldgracepublishinghouse.com

Dedication

To Nathan and Olivia
Bratianu who bring
so much joy to my life.

Dear . . . .

I am
Dominick the Mouse.
And I
live in your house.

Sometimes when you sleep, I sneak into the kitchen for cookies and cheese.

I love to jump around, and play with your toys.

To sneak under
the blankets,
and tickle your toes.

As you can see,

I'm not that big.

I'm small and cute.

And we can
be friends,
if you want to.

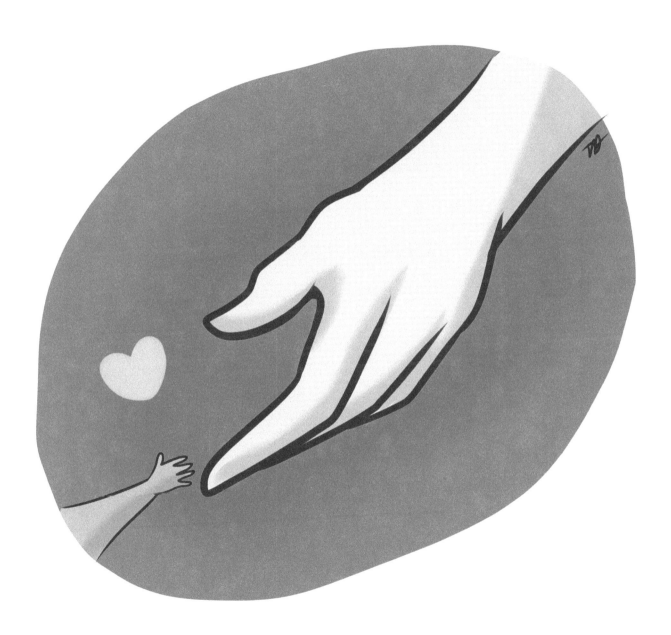

*I can read you stories,
and cuddle
with you at night.*

Be your best friend,
and play
ZIG-ZAG-ZANG!

I could also help you brush your teeth and hair.

And pick up
your toys
from everywhere.

I am Dominick
the Mouse!
And now,
what's your name?

So........., what do you say?

Do you want
to be best friends?

With love,

Dominick the Mouse

Squeak! Squeak! Squeak!

About the Author

Daniela Elena was a Sunday School teacher who loves children. She studied art and music in school and plays piano and cello.

Daniela is also an avid supporter of Anti-Human Trafficking Awareness. In addition she has started her own business, Classy Closets by Daniela.

Daniela is very creative and inspired by children. She has many stories to tell and will be publishing them soon.

Visit Daniela on Facebook at:
www.facebook.com/Daniela Elena